OP

States of
Matter
Liquids

Maria Koran

EYEDISCOVER

EYEDISCOVER

Go to **www.eyediscover.com** and enter this book's unique code.

BOOK CODE

V992998

EYEDISCOVER brings you optic readalongs that support active learning.

Published by AV² by Weigl
350 5th Avenue, 59th Floor   New York, NY   10118
Website: www.eyediscover.com

Library of Congress Control Number: 2016946710

ISBN 978-1-4896-5183-9 (hardcover)

Printed in the United States of America
in Brainerd, Minnesota
1 2 3 4 5 6 7 8 9 0 20 19 18 17 16

072016
040716

Project Coordinator: Warren Rylands
Designer: Mandy Christiansen

Weigl acknowledges iStock, Getty Images, Corbis, and Shutterstock as the primary image suppliers for this title.

EYEDISCOVER provides enriched content, optimized for tablet use, that supplements and complements this book. EYEDISCOVER books strive to create inspired learning and engage young minds in a total learning experience.

I am a lion.

Watch
Video content brings each page to life.

Browse
Thumbnails make navigation simple.

Read
Follow along with text on the screen.

Listen
Hear each page read aloud.

Your EYEDISCOVER Optic Readalongs come alive with...

Audio
Listen to the entire book read aloud.

Video
High resolution videos turn each spread into an optic readalong.

OPTIMIZED FOR

☑ **TABLETS**

☑ **WHITEBOARDS**

☑ **COMPUTERS**

☑ **AND MUCH MORE!**

Liquids

In this book, you will learn about

- **what they are**

- **how they change**

- **how they feel**

and much more!

Liquids are one kind of matter. Liquids have no shape, but they take up space.

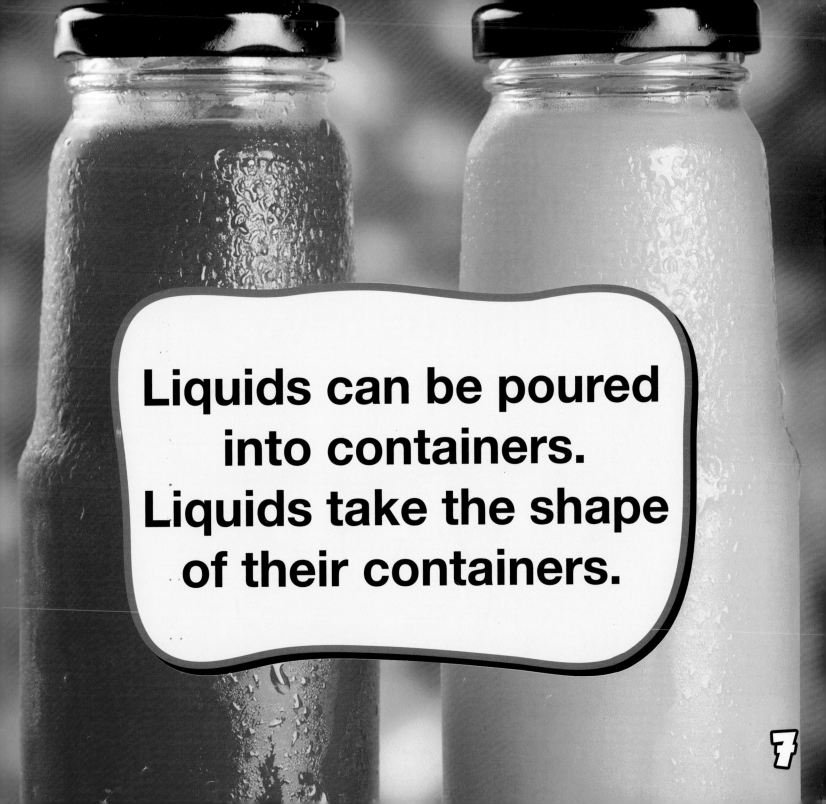

Liquids can be poured into containers. Liquids take the shape of their containers.

The way a liquid feels is called its texture. Liquids have different textures.

8

10

Some liquids
are thick.

13

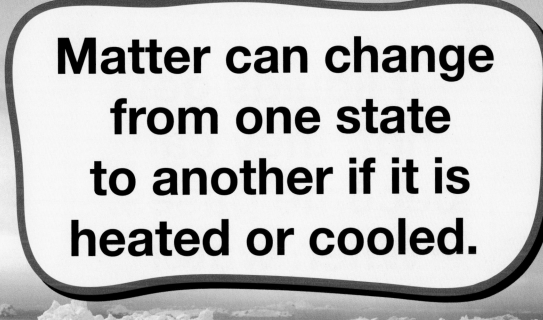

Matter can change from one state to another if it is heated or cooled.

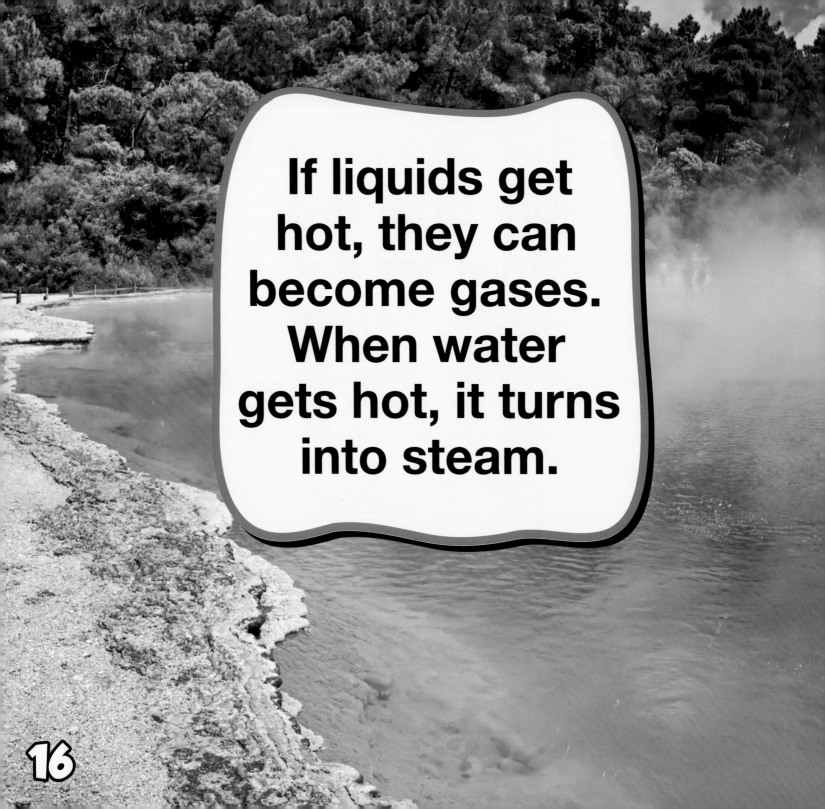

If liquids get hot, they can become gases. When water gets hot, it turns into steam.

17

18

Liquids can become solids when they get cold. When water gets cold, it turns into ice.

19

Water is one of the most important liquids on Earth. It can be found in many places.

21

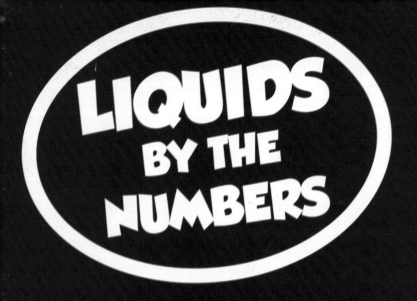

LIQUIDS BY THE NUMBERS

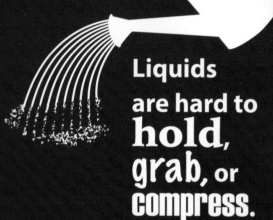

Liquids are hard to **hold, grab,** or **compress.**

Liquid water makes up **60** to **80%** of the human body.

Liquids are runny and they **flow** *downwards.*

The lava of a volcano is a liquid.

71% of Earth's surface is water-covered.

Liquids can CHANGE SHAPE depending on the containers they are in.

Water turns to ice at 32° Fahrenheit.
(0° Celsius)

KEY WORDS

Research has shown that as much as 65 percent of all written material published in English is made up of 300 words. These 300 words cannot be taught using pictures or learned by sounding them out. They must be recognized by sight. This book contains 41 common sight words to help young readers improve their reading fluency and comprehension. This book also teaches young readers several important content words, such as proper nouns. These words are paired with pictures to aid in learning and improve understanding.

Page	Sight Words First Appearance	Page	Content Words First Appearance
4	are, but, have, kind, no, or, one, take, they, up	4	liquids, matter, shape, space
7	be, can, into, the, their	7	containers
8	a, different, is, its, way	8	texture
11	some	16	gases, steam
15	another, change, from, if, it, or, state, to	19	ice, solids
16	get, turns, water, when		
20	Earth, found, important, in, many, most, on, places		

I am a lion.

Watch
Video content brings each page to life.

Browse
Thumbnails make navigation simple.

Read
Follow along with text on the screen.

Listen
Hear each page read aloud.

EYEDISCOVER

Go to **www.eyediscover.com** and enter this book's unique code.

BOOK CODE

V992998